Reading Together

Once Upon a Time

Read it together

The pictures in *Once Upon a Time* bring together many favourite stories and nursery rhymes. Yet the words tell another story, about a boy's day where nothing much seems to happen, or so he says!

The humour in this book depends on children's familiarity with traditional rhymes and stories.

> I like this story best.

> Who's this over here?

> It's the three pigs building their house!

Children will enjoy being "experts", identifying familiar characters and discovering the secrets and jokes inside this book.

> Daddy's washing up. I look out. Is that someone walking about?

The gentle rhyme helps children to remember how the story goes. They may want to read it to you. Don't worry if the words aren't always the same as those on the page. They will become more accurate with time.

If they are reading and get stuck on a word, show them how to guess what it says by:
- looking at the pictures
- looking at the letter the word begins with
- reading the rest of the sentence and coming back to it.

Always help them if they get really stuck or tired by giving them the word.

Children will notice more about the way letters and words look by writing them down. Help them to write some of the words they know well, like family names.

This picture book offers lots to talk about. Children might wonder why the boy in the story can see all the different characters but his parents can't!

We hope you enjoy reading this book together.

For Jasmine

First published 1993
by Walker Books Ltd
87 Vauxhall Walk
London SE11 5HJ

This edition published 1998

4 6 8 10 9 7 5 3

Text © 1993 Vivian French
Illustrations © 1993 John Prater
Introductory and concluding notes © 1998 CLPE

Printed in Great Britain

ISBN 0-7445-5701-1

Once Upon a Time

Conceived and illustrated by
John Prater

Text by
Vivian French

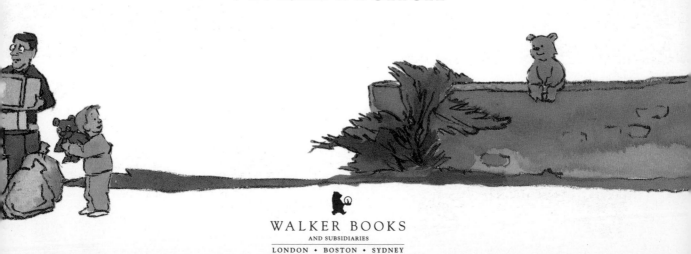

WALKER BOOKS
AND SUBSIDIARIES

LONDON · BOSTON · SYDNEY

Early in the morning
Cat and me.

Not much to do.
Not much to see.

Dad's off to work now
Mum's up too.

Not much to see.
Not much to do.

Day's getting older
Sun's up high.

Wave to a little girl
Hurrying by.

Mum's cleaning windows.
Here's a bear

Making a fuss
About a chair.

Ride my tricycle
For a while.

There's an egg
With a happy smile.

Mum's in the garden.
Washing's dry.

Why do babies
Always cry?

We've got sandwiches –
Cheese today.

Why's that wolf saying
"Come this way"?

I like jumping
To and fro.

That wolf's howling –
He's hurt his toe.

Mum's drinking coffee.
We can chat.

I tell her my jump
Is as big as THAT!

Here's Dad home again!
Time for tea.

I wave to him
And he waves to me.

Dad's washing dishes.
I look out.

Did I hear someone
Walking about?

Time for my story.
I yawn and say,

"Nothing much happened
Round here today."

Read it again

There are many well-known stories and rhymes in this book. You can enjoy looking back through the pictures to tell the tale of each set of characters in turn. You could also find and read the original versions of these stories and rhymes.

The Family
What happens to the little boy's cat?

The Three Little Pigs
Who wants to blow their house in?

Goldilocks and the Three Bears
Who mends the broken chair?

The Witch
Why does she
get cross?

The Giant
Whose tail does
he tread on?

Hey Diddle
Diddle
Can you sing
the song about the
cat and the fiddle?

Humpty Dumpty
Can you say a rhyme
about him?

Red Riding Hood
What happens
to her?

Reading Together

The *Reading Together* series is divided into four levels – starting with red, then on to yellow, blue and finally green. The six books in each level offer children varied experiences of reading. There are stories, poems, rhymes and songs, traditional tales and information books to choose from.

Accompanying the series is a Parents' Handbook, which looks at all the different ways children learn to read and explains how *your* help can really make a difference!

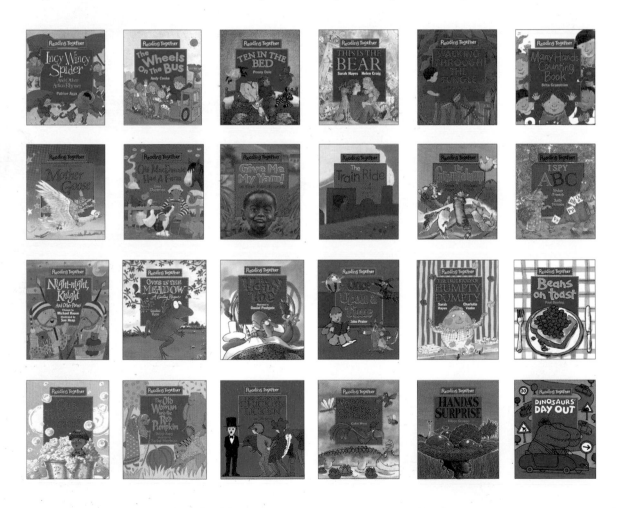